The Man in the Moon-Fixer's Mask

by JonArno Lawson

illustrated by Sherwin Tjia

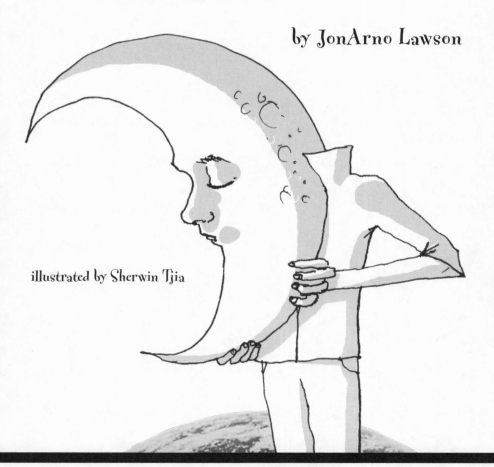

The Man in the Moon-Fixer's Mask

by JonArno Lawson

illustrated by Sherwin Tjia

Pedlar Press | Toronto

PEDLAR PRESS
PO Box 26, Station P, Toronto Ontario M5S 2S6 Canada

ACKNOWLEDGEMENTS. The publisher gratefully acknowledges the
financial support of the Canada Council for the Arts and the Ontario
Arts Council for its publishing program.

NATIONAL LIBRARY OF CANADA CATALOGUING IN
PUBLICATION

Lawson, JonArno
    The man in the moon-fixer's mask / JonArno Lawson; Sherwin Tjia,
illustrator.

Poems.
ISBN 0-9732140-9-0

    1. Children's poetry, Canadian (English) I. Tjia, Sherwin, 1975–
II. Title.

PS8573.A93M35 2004   C811'.54   C2004-902081-1

First Edition

DESIGN Zab Design & Typography
TYPEFACE (Headings) *Fontesque*, designed by Nick Shinn

Printed in Canada

For Sophie and Asher – an adventure begins

Contents

The Man in the Moon-Fixer's Mask

Mope

The Mope I knew
was without hope.

She moped and moped.
I hoped and hoped

some happy thought might help her cope.
Did my hopes help her moping? Nope.

Slouch

How very bad it is to slouch
at the dining room table, on the arm of a couch

and if you maintain this asocial position
it won't be too long till they phone a physician

and you'll be confined to a hospital bed
where they'll tie up your shoulders and strap up your head.

So you'd better listen and not be a grouch
when for your own good you are told not to slouch.

The Empty-Headed Scarecrow

The empty-headed scarecrow comes
at night
with blood-red rhubarb stalks
to pummel hollow pumpkin drums.

Its burlap voice is dry as straw
that rasps and hums with cricket songs –
cicada trills, the buzz of flies,
and black-shelled rustling beetle throngs.

At dawn it stops
the rooster crows
then starts
the far-off bark of dogs:

Quick up the post –
While in its empty head it learns
next nighttime's drumming
from a clotted gonging
organ-throated pond of frogs.

The Slowpoke Vogue

The slowpoke slogged along then stopped.
I never saw the slowpoke hop
or skip. His feet were always bound
by slowpoke habits to the ground.

It made me mad. I had to speak:
"Why do you walk so slow, you rogue?"
His answer seemed to take a week.
"Me? I'm a slowpoke, it's in vogue."

She Crept Across the Crevice

She crept across the crevice with criminal intent,
but when she stood upright she found her urge to injure went.

Where had it gone? She lay back down
and crept again over the crack –

And indeed near the ground, she suddenly found
that her devilish thoughts came back.

A Princess Apprentice

A princess apprentice
a prince oppressed
a duke undecided
a duchess undressed

The Great Snoth of Snitch-on-the-Snotch

I met the Great Snoth of Snitch-on-the-Snotch,
drinking tea from a seashell while winding his watch.
"My goodness," said he, when he finally looked up,
"what an odd little creature I have for a cup."

Vincent the Vanisher

Oh where did poor Vincent
the Vanisher go?
He vanished so quickly
that nobody knows.

Of Vincent the Vanisher
none can keep track.
He knows how to vanish
but not how to come back.

He'll only appear long enough
to proclaim,
"I'm Vincent the Vanisher,
that is my name.

"I can vanish quite easily.
What I can't seem to learn
is why once I've vanished
I never return."

Then before any expert
can come to advise
he's starting to
dematerialize.

Vincent oh Vincent,
oh why do you lack
the knowledge of how,
once you've gone, to come back?

The Itibar of Ilm

The Itibar of Ilm looked in a mirror –
And there he saw the Ilm of Itibar.

"Is that me?" (The fear he underwent!)
"Me that is," he heard, and felt content.

Gazdiks in the Gond

The Gazdiks came from far away
by foot by wheel and wave,
too restless for this great green world,
too restless for the grave.

They never had to stir themselves,
they bristled at the brinks.
"We're Gazdiks – please don't stir us –
we are humans, we're not drinks."

The Gazdiks found a funny thing
out somewhere in the Gond,
but they never said exactly where they found
the money pond.

– Frogs that chuffed and croaked on nickels
– Dragonflies with wings of dime
– The mud a crush of copper pennies
– Reeds like quarters stacked in shafts

From Tracadie to Trebizond,
to Tallahassee and beyond,
explorers seek the money pond.
But ask the Gazdiks where it is

they smile and don't respond.
Ask them again, they whisper,
"Son, it's somewhere in the Gond,
look within it – not beyond."

Great-Grandpa Glen

Great-Grandpa Glen
was angry when
a busy busload beeped at him.
He parked his car
to block the street
and stopped all the traffic in Hamilton.

Aghast

Aghast that a guest was a ghost,
a fellow guest goaded the host –
The gist of it was
he was angry because
a gust from a ghost chilled his toast.

Ella-Bella

Poor little Ella-Bella,
five years old,
does the dishes every morning
just as she is told.

Little Palmer

Little Palmer has a pair
of Palomino skates.
He skates the Hudson nightly
near New Hamburg's city gates.

To Catch a Witch

To catch a witch,
first make a wish,
then quietly go put a dish
of dandelions in a ditch.

Rub some ashes on your chin,
tie a feather to your shin.
Draw a circle with some chalk
(that will give a nasty shock
to any witch who wishes to
cast a nasty spell on you!).

Invite her for a glass of sherry
then offer up a magic cherry.
When she eats it, take her shoe
and give it to a dog to chew.

With all of this correctly done,
you'll have no trouble, you'll have won.
But now you'll need a pleasant room
in which to keep her and her broom.

And every day
you'll need to feed her,
so before you catch her,
make sure you need her.

The Purpose of the Porpoise

"The purpose of the porpoise?
Its preposterous propensity
for spinning on its nose odd props,
regardless of their density."

The porpoise heard and said,
"Why do you propagate such tales?
Do you promulgate such rot
on the proclivities of whales?"

The Rhinostrich

With a beak and a horn –
Yes I know it's a stretch –
But imagine when born
what a price she would fetch.

With her leathery feathers
and hide-covered eggs,
with two wings, two thick-set,
and two skinny legs,

I want a rhinostrich
whatever the price.
And I'd never sell her –
it wouldn't be nice.

The Badger, the Barn Fowl and Their Little Friend the Snail

My love, I see you sitting
scribbling nonsense in a book.
I can tell you are not happy,
it's apparent in your look.
Perhaps you will permit me
to relate a little tale
about a badger and a barn fowl
and their little friend the snail.

The three of them sat talking
until late into the night.
The badger snarled and growled,
sometimes he gave the others fright.
"Peep Peep!" the barn fowl squeaked,
she was a feather-headed sight.
But the snail kept very cool
and slowly wound himself up tight.

The badger told the others
how he once had been in love.
"Too bad it was a bird," he said,
"a pretty turtledove,
but she turned up her beak at me,
that creature of the air.
There's no way she would live, she said,
in some poor badger's lair."

The snail had been in love as well;
he told them with remorse
how he had fallen badly
for a proud and stately horse.
"She mistook me for an acorn
and I very nearly died,"
said their little friend, the snail,
as he unwound again and cried.

"At least," piped up the barn fowl,
"you are not loved by a rooster."
It was quite true - he crowed and hopped
in circles, which confused her.
"I'd rather live alone than with
that noisy circling bird."
Then she ruffled up her fluff
and would not say another word.

My love, I think it best now that
we leave these weeping three
to their tales of their lost loves
and to their love of misery.

Horses in Cities

Good and iniquitous,
they were ubiquitous:
Horses were everywhere
anyone looked.
But with cars, numbers dwindled,
and sightings diminished,
and then one day horses in cities
were finished.

On Admiral Road

On Admiral Road,
there lives a toad
who likes to sing of the things
he's owed.

He's owed a little
or owed a load.
"It depends on the day,"
sings the odious toad.

The odious tiny
melodious toad.

The Hippopossum

Beneath that bougainvillea blossom,
behold my friends, the hippopossum.

He got the best of Mom and Dad,
but good in them, in him, is bad.

Sleepy, stocky, awkward, awesome –
He'll eat anything you toss him.

Curse him and you may feel glad
he's lazy; but I wouldn't cross him.

My Garden Breeds a Savage Bloom

My garden breeds a savage bloom,
deep-rooted in the loam,
and from the safety of my room
I watch it guard my home.

I like how it intimidates
each nose who stoops to sniff it.
I contemplate the doom awaiting
him who stops to pick it.

It's frighteningly pink.
It stops all idle chatter.
It forces fools to think
(though thinkers' thoughts no longer matter).

Under the glowering
goat-lidded loom
of my garden's
savage bloom.

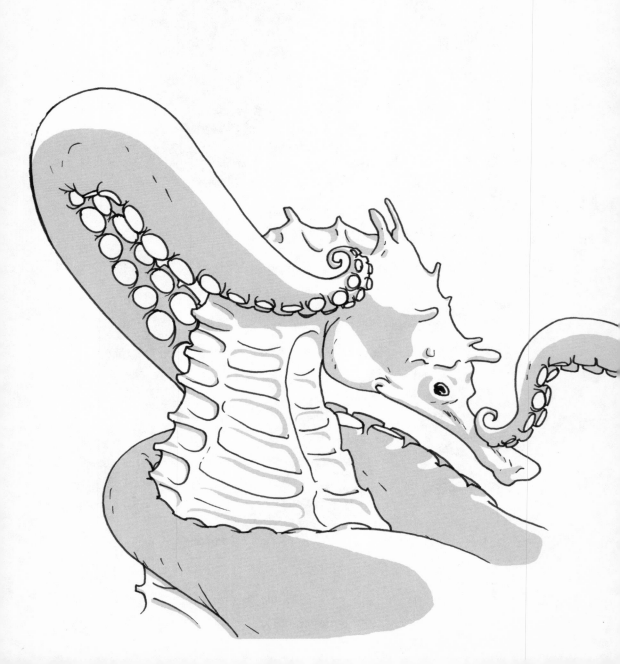

The Octopus and the Seahorse

The seahorse bowed to the octopus
and asked if she would please
join him in his nighttime dance
around the coral keys.
Her shyness put his aquatic
quasi-equestrian heart at ease.
She blinked her eye and then she bowed,
bending her many knees.

They danced, they danced –
the Octopus-Seahorse dance –
in their many-legged
multi-coloured barnacle-covered pants.
They danced, they danced –
and their twirling was much enhanced
by the current above the seabed floor
and their oceanic trance.

The Common Cowl

Are you mammal, are you fowl?
Offspring of the cow
and owl?

Anomalous you may be now.
Uncommon we may want to keep you.
But let another handsome owl

meet another comely cow
and soon we'll all be very used to
meeting with the Common cowl.

The Rabbit and the Rhino

The hidden rabbit was habit-ridden,
stopping only when it hopped into places safely hidden.
But it plopped in its haste through a rhino's yawning jaws
and went skittering down his throat on her slippery little paws.

The wise old crow went crazy with woe
when he saw the rhino swallowing the rabbit so.
He crowed, "Little rhino, let the rabbit go,"
but the rhino said, "No, I don't have to, old crow."

Now the rabbit got restless and she wanted to get out,
and the rhino's belly ached from the wiggling of her snout.
So the little rhino strained with an angry little pout
and he opened up his jaws and the rabbit hopped out.

The Snake

The kiss of a snake
arrives at the tip
of a double-pronged tongue.

So make no mistake:
If a kiss has two tips
instead of two lips

you'd better run.

United Bakers

When we eat at United Bakers,
don't take the salt and pepper shakers
and shake them down our backs.

When we eat at United Bakers,
please don't tear the sugar packs
or pour the ketchup down our backs.

When we eat at United Bakers,
please eat more than fries and ice:
A tuna reuben would be nice

when we eat at United Bakers.

Jimmy Spitnickles

Jimmy Spitnickles
was not fond of tickles.
Whenever the tickles came near,
he twisted and turned
like a slippery pickle
and screamed so loud no one could hear.
But the tickles that travelled
in fingers unravelled
around him in spite of his fear.

Togo Salmon Hall

Who works in Togo Salmon Hall?
Bob, Karl, Fritz and Jerry.
Do any work in Chester New?
The cellar there is scary.

Who works in Togo Salmon Hall?
Gerhart, Hans and Jim.
And Martin, many years ago,
but few remember him –

On a whim Martin went into Chester New's cellar,
improbably armed with an airplane propeller,
seeking the feared subterranean dweller –

But the lighting was terribly dim –
and it seems what was down there found him –
for we never saw Martin again.

The Snail

A snail looks something like a knuckle,
pretzled and bent about into a buckle –
because its spiralling nature makes it
go wherever its twisting takes it.

Hippopotamus

We saw a hippopotamus;
I don't know what it thought of us.
I doubt it thought a lot of us;
a glimpse was all it got of us.

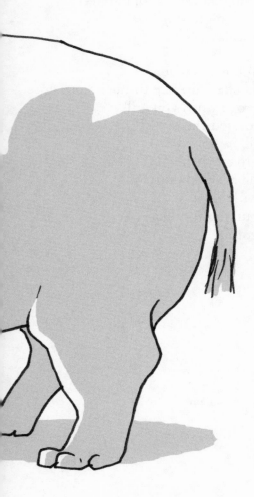

Still a Gorilla

You may bake
like a snake,
or bat
like a cat,
sing
like a herring,
or pat
like a bat –
but you're still a
gorilla.

You may scowl
like an owl,
or box
like a fox,
disturb us with snorts
like an ox
when he talks –
but you're still a
gorilla.

You may feel
like an eel,
or fail
like a whale,
have the habits
of rabbits

or the snout
of a snail,
the remorse
of a horse
who takes the wrong trail –
but you're still a
gorilla.

You may vacuum
vanilla fumes up through your nose,
growl when you grill
toasted cheese
till it glows,
groan when you
fill a balloon up
with blows –
but you're still a
gorilla.

An Ibis

An Ibis
whose tribe is
restricted in range
will find
new encounters
disruptive and strange.

The Frog Knows His Prognosis

The frog meets a heron
alone in the wood,
the frog knows his prognosis
is not very good.
If he could leap clear
then he certainly would.

The Dip of a Bat

The dip of a bat
or the tip of a hat?
An elegant pump
or an elephant rump?
A head that's been shrunken
or a ship that's been sunken?

We'll be here all night
if we bungle it right.

A valuable necklace
or a snake who's been reckless?
A dragon who roars
or a grandpa who snores?
A muttering ghost
or a shuddering post?

It's all very frightening
and not that enlightening.

The hem of a skirt
or a hen in the dirt?
A menacing heap
or a child asleep?
The teeth of a shark
or a fence in the dark?

It was all making sense
till that shark and that fence.

And if we don't somehow
soon come to our senses,
sorting the sharks in the dark
from the fences,
we'll certainly suffer
some grave consequences.

The Sock-Seeker

The sock-seeker sought
for her socks in a sack.
She was off to play soccer –
her soccer mates sat

in a circle to savour
a pre-soccer chat,
sipping Schweppes out of saucers
on exercise mats.

When she showed up re-socked
from her soccer-socks sack,
they said, "Sally, you're late,
but your stockings – they match!"

The Doubtful

I've skirmished and skirted,
I've sputtered and sped,
I've skittered and scuttered
and spun on my head.

Skedaddling paddling rattling about,
I've tugged at the tail of a troublesome trout.
I've stymied a sniff that was snuffling out.
I've murmured and whispered; I've stifled a shout.

But that's all I've done
that I've done without doubt.
There are the things that I've done
some are doubtful about –
To comfort the doubtful
I've left those things out.

I Spun

I spun
where I was told to spin
and while I spun
grabbed hold of him
who told me
where I had to spin.
I could tell
it startled him.

Should I Be Me?

Who's who?
I'm me.
You're you.

We're we.
He's he.
She's she.

So tell us
what to do –

Should he be she?
Should she be he?
Should I be me
or you?

On Harbord Street

On Harbord Street
I slow my feet.
I'd like to rush.
How can I though?

The sights and smells of Harbord Street
are tugging at my eyes and nose –
the library, the bakery, the bookstores there. . .
Old men who doze

on Harbord Street
are luckier than kings and those
who doze away in golden clothes
in palaces and bungalows

who've never dreamed of libraries
and bakeries and bookstores,
like the ones they have on Harbord Street.
What books to read! What sweets to eat!

She Took Two Rings

She took two rings
and grabbed her gown,
and rode her bike to Chinatown
– Toronto's much like China
at Dundas and Spadina –

and there she grabbed
her groom-to-be
from the desk
of a Chinese grocery.

If you want to see it
I'll show you for free –
it was caught on
a secret surveillance TV.

So he swung up onto her handlebars
and they wove about between the cars.
Forhewan! Cumbolagabrecken!, she'd say
to any poor soul who got in their way.

In a bit they arrived
at a place pre-arranged
where the groom stayed the same
but the bride-to-be changed.

Then they promised each other
they'd never betray
any vows that they happened
to make on that day.

Then they vowed to be quiet,
if that's what it took,
to allow one another
to finish a book.

(And they vowed to be cautious
whenever they'd meet
if one had on shoes
and the other bare feet.)

Yes they pledged and they promised,
they promised and swore.
Then they took a short break
and they promised some more.

And they wrote it all down on a popsicle stick
and gave it one last loving lingering lick
and then buried it under the Wychwood Yard brick.

The Man In The Moon-Fixer's Mask

The moon fell down
and bounce by bounce
it lost its substance
ounce by ounce.

"My heavens," it murmured,
"I'm in big trouble,
though I am still the moon
not a poppable bubble."

The unstoppable bouncing
was jolting the world.
What wasn't tied down
shook loose and unfurled.

The oceans were heaving,
the sky was a mess,
there were clouds on the ground,
there was east in the west.

No one knew how to do
this impossible task –
To put the moon back!
No one knew who to ask.

Then someone appeared
in a moon-fixer's mask.
"Allow me," he said,
"to get on with my task."

Then he tenderly tucked the moon
back in its orbit.
Well if it wasn't
Geoffrey James Ivan Corbet,
I'm really not sure who it was.

The Matrix Restaurant

He was washing the dishes,
a man with eyelashes
so long they could butter your toast.
He said, "Though I know it sounds hard to believe,
long ago I was wealthier than most.
Though now you may see me and know me and treat me
as down-and-out dishwasher Sam,
hardly more than what now seems a moment ago
I was known as the King of Siam."

I know – though it sounds improbable –
Sam showed us his former crown.
I was busy with tables of dinner-time customers
or else I would have knelt down.

Marleena the waitress –
our boss at the Matrix –
was a woman who'd seen all the world.
She said, "Listen Sam, I was Queen of the Coffee Shop parties
when I was a girl.
Though now I serve eggs,
the sight of my legs
once caused every man's moustache to curl.
I may seem like an ordinary woman to you,
but I wasn't an ordinary girl."

I know – though it sounds unlikely –
Marleena the waitress began
to dance the way she used to dance in the days
when old Sam was the King of Siam.

The chef who'd been listening quietly
suddenly started to speak while he cooked.
"Oh mother, Oh father, I knew that I'd find you –
I knew it someday if I looked.
I was told that my Mom was a Queen, and a dancer
at parties when she was a girl,
and my Dad was the King of Siam and
at one time the wealthiest man in the world."

I know – though it sounds incredible –
Marleena, Sam and the cook,
when looked at again in the light of this news
had a strikingly similar look.

Talking in the Caucasus

If you plan to climb mountains or even go walking
between the Caspian and the Black Sea,
you may need to learn some brand new ways of talking,
so let me prepare you for what these might be:

You may need to know Abkhaz, Abaza or Akhwakh,
Avar and Andi or Agul and Archi
Or maybe Armenian and Azerbaijani,
Balkar, Bezhita (sometimes known as Kapuchi).

Bagvalal, Batsbi, Botlikh and Budukh,
there's Chechen and Chamalal,
also Circassian (some use Cherkess and some Kabardin),
Dargwa and Greek, Godoberi, Ginukh,

Georgian and Hunzib, Ingush, Karata
Khaidaq and Khinalug, Kurdish, Khwarshi,
Kumyk and Kryz, Karachay, Kubachi,
Lezgi and Lak, Mingrelian, Nogay,

Ossetian and Russian, Rutul and Svan
Tabasaran, Tindi, Turkomen, Tat.
Talysh, Tsez, Tsakhur,
Ukrainian and Udi.

And all of this talking is done in the main
in an area not one bit larger than Spain.
So if this is where you would like to go walk,
learn some of these so, while you're there, you can talk.

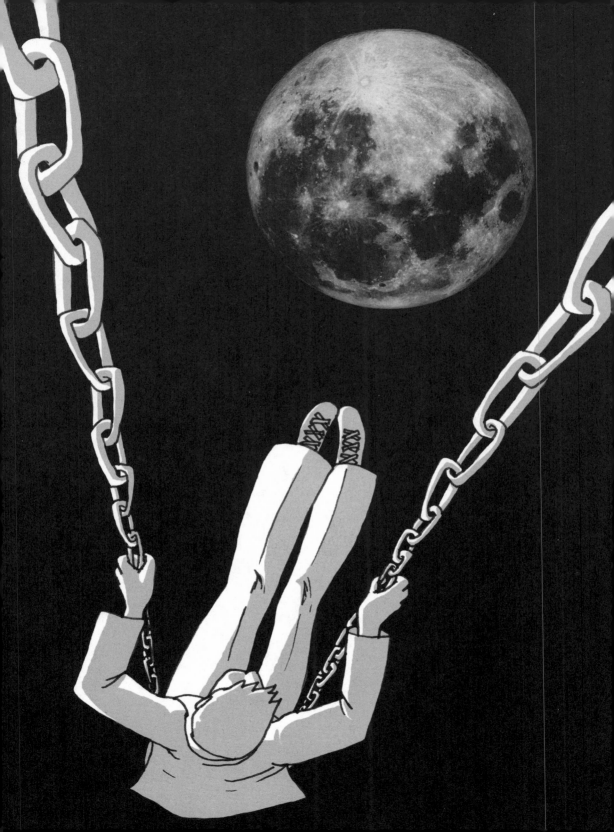

The Dundas Driving Park

Down to the Dundas Driving Park,
my tires are cutting the puddles in half.
There's wind in my hair and it makes me laugh.
There's rain and the street lights buzz in the dark
and I'm on my way to the driving park.

There's a wading pool in the driving park,
and a tunnel made from a sewer pipe,
and the moon's full of milk and the stars are ripe,
and the grass is wet and my feet are bare
and I cling to my swing as it flies through the air.

Not a moment to lose in the driving park.
There's a jungle gym like a rocket ship
and a teeter-totter where I once tore
the very top of my fingertip.
There may be others who go there more
by day, I really can't be sure.

I race down at night through the rain in the dark
to my wind-blown dreams in the driving park.

JONARNO LAWSON is the author of two less light-hearted books of poetry and aphorisms: *Love is an Observant Traveller* and *Inklings*, as well as a contributor to *The Chechens: A Handbook* edited by Amjad Jaimoukha. He lives in Toronto with his wife and two children.

ACKNOWLEDGEMENTS

Thanks to Amy, Sophie and Asher – la mia favoloso famiglia – who were my first listeners and editors. To Beth Follett for her gifts, great ideas and careful editing. To the Major Ballachey School "I Am" Autumn Poetry Workshop Anthology, 2003, in which "The Sock-Seeker" first appeared, and to Ada, Myra, Gertrude and Hazel Burhans, long-deceased, the true authors of "Ella-Bella" (a teasing rhyme used to taunt my grandmother in the late 1800s.) Thanks very much also to Jessy Kahn, Jim and Glen Lawson, Sharon Zikman and Michael, Alex and Zachary Levine, Tami, Mike, Elle, Macy and Jett Armstrong, Rachelle Sender and Ron Lancaster for looking at the manuscript and providing useful comments and suggestions, to Stephen for pointing me back to Beth, and to fabulous Zab for her Midas touch. A very special thanks to Sherwin Tjia for his illustrative genius and for all the added dimensions that come with it.